Dear Parents:

Congratulations! Your child is taking the first steps on an exciting journey. The destination? Independent reading!

STEP INTO READING® will help your child get there. The program offers five steps to reading success. Each step includes fun stories and colorful art or photographs. In addition to original fiction and books with favorite characters, there are Step into Reading Non-Fiction Readers, Phonics Readers and Boxed Sets, Sticker Readers, and Comic Readers—a complete literacy program with something to interest every child.

Learning to Read, Step by Step!

Ready to Read   Preschool–Kindergarten
• big type and easy words • rhyme and rhythm • picture clues
For children who know the alphabet and are eager to begin reading.

Reading with Help   Preschool–Grade 1
• basic vocabulary • short sentences • simple stories
For children who recognize familiar words and sound out new words with help.

Reading on Your Own   Grades 1–3
• engaging characters • easy-to-follow plots • popular topics
For children who are ready to read on their own.

Reading Paragraphs   Grades 2–3
• challenging vocabulary • short paragraphs • exciting stories
For newly independent readers who read simple sentences with confidence.

Ready for Chapters   Grades 2–4
• chapters • longer paragraphs • full-color art
For children who want to take the plunge into chapter books but still like colorful pictures.

STEP INTO READING® is designed to give every child a successful reading experience. The grade levels are only guides; children will progress through the steps at their own speed, developing confidence in their reading.

Remember, a lifetime love of reading starts with a single step!

Visit us on the Web!
StepIntoReading.com
rhcbooks.com

Educators and librarians, for a variety of teaching tools, visit us at RHTeachersLibrarians.com

ISBN 978-1-9848-4807-9 (trade) — ISBN 978-1-9848-4808-6 (lib. bdg.)

Printed in the United States of America

10 9 8 7 6 5 4 3 2 1

A Toy for Trinket

adapted by Kristen L. Depken

based on the teleplay
"Trinket's Toy Trouble" by Kerri Gran

illustrated by Marcela Cespedes-Alicea

Random House 🏠 New York

Nella and Trinket have a lot of stuff they do not use anymore.

They will give it away!

Trinket sees her baby toy.

She wants to keep it.

She does not want
her friends to think
she is a baby.
She puts it back.

Griffin finds the toy.

He will use it

to wash his dishes.

Oh, no!
Trinket wants her
toy back!

Nella will help.

They will find Griffin.

Splash!

They cross a mud puddle.

Thunk!

Nella hits

pine cones away.

Whoosh!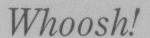

Nella swings after Griffin.

She cannot

catch up to him.

Griffin goes home
to Windy Point Peaks.
Nella and Trinket follow.
They ride the wind up!

The friends find Griffin.
Trinket asks him
for her toy back.

Griffin says yes.

He has a baby toy, too!

He understands.

Trinket is so happy!

Nella makes Griffin

a new brush

for his dishes.

Griffin gives the friends
a ride home.

Trinket does not care
what her friends think.
She loves her toy!